for all my little jett-pups, with love -
lael, oliver m, oliver s, iola, leif, sivan, maya,
tatiana, hayden, portia and carrie.

Channel Photographics Publishing
980 Lincoln Ave. Suite 200 B
San Rafael California, 94901
T: 415.456.2934 F: 415. 456.4124

www.channelphotographics.com

ISBN-13: 978-0-9773399-7-6

US/Canadian Distribution -
Publishers Group West
1700 Fourth Street,
Berkeley, CA 94710
T: 877.528.1444

Illustrations and Text Copyright –
David Gordon

Printed and bound in China
by Global PSD
www.globalpsd.com

Channel Photographics & Global Printing,
Sourcing & Development (Global PSD), in
association with American Forests and the
Global ReLeaf programs, will plant two trees for
each tree used in the manufacturing of this book.
Global ReLeaf is an international campaign by
American Forests, the nation's oldest nonprofit
conservation organization and a world leader in
planting trees for environmental restoration.

Replanted
Paper

Jett
-pup

written and illustrated by david gordon

Your new JETT-pup will arrive in a single, nicely packed wooden crate.

All the parts shown easily snap together.

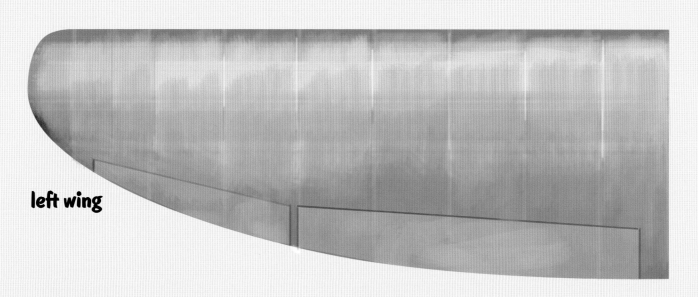

left wing

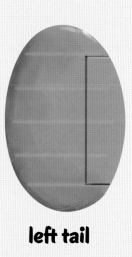

left tail

right wing

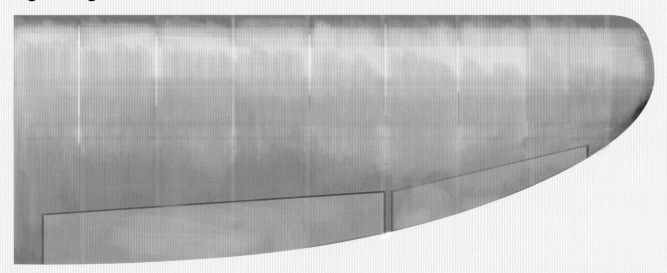

right tail

And JETT-pup comes mostly pre-assembled...

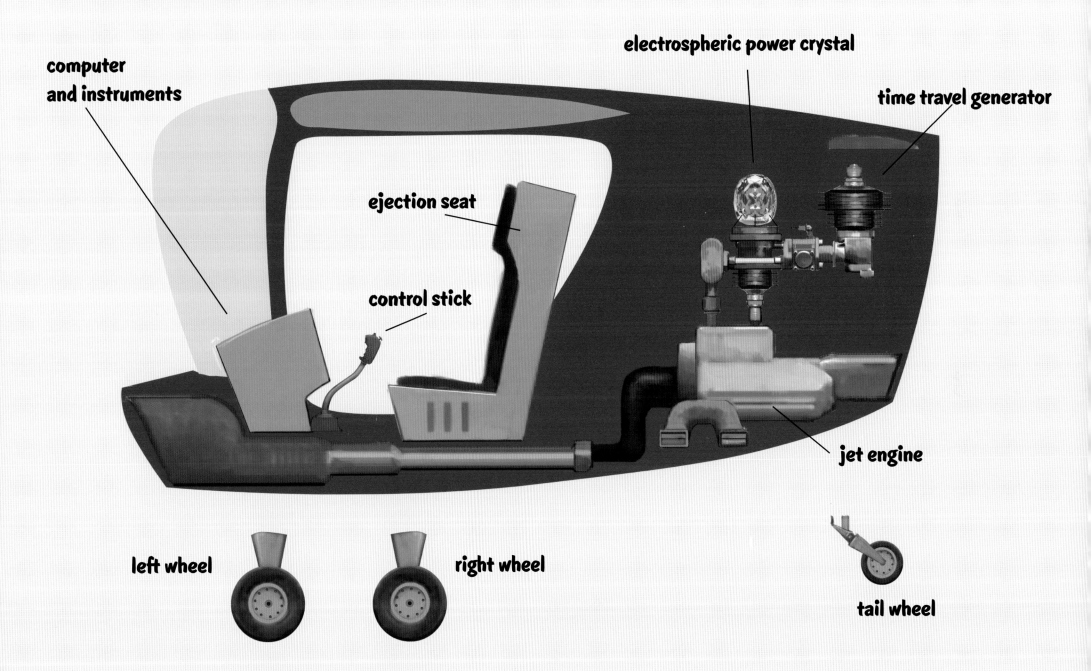

computer and instruments

electrospheric power crystal

time travel generator

ejection seat

control stick

jet engine

left wheel

right wheel

tail wheel

Control Stick

The all-important control stick. Push it forward and JETT-pup
will go down. Pull it back, JETT-pup
will go up.
Move it to your right (starboard),
and left (port) to turn
JETT-pup left and right.

Auto Pilot:
Push this and JETT-pup will
fly itself.

Trigger:
Pull trigger to launch stuffed animals
from the stuffed animal gun.

**Thumb control for communications
and music:**
Pull it back or push it forward to
increase or decrease volume in your
helmet speakers, left and right to
scroll through songs or
people you want to talk to.

The Cockpit

Altitude Indicator:
Tells you how high you are,
up to 100,000 feet.

Air Speed Indicator:
Tells you how fast you're going,
up to 1000 mph.

Year:
Set these three switches to
time travel to the month,
day and year you want.
You can go up to tens of
millions of years into the
past or future.

Throttle:
Makes the JETT-pup speed
up or slow down. Push
the red button to hover.

Attitude Indicator:
Tells you if you're tilting left or right, up
or down relative to the horizon.

Compass:
Tells you which direction you're
going. North, East,
South and West.

Start Button:
Push this after you flip the
Power switch to UP.

EJECT! Button:
For emergencies
only!!!

Left Rudder Pedal:
Helps JETT-pup go to
the left.

Right Rudder Pedal:
Helps JETT-pup go to
the right.

Invisidoor Switch:
Flip this up to close the
invisible doors.

Landing Lights

Navigation Wing Lights:
Red (port - left)
Blue (starboard - right)

Parking Brake

Flaps:
Pull back to make the flaps go down, push
forward to make them go up. The flaps
are those flappy things on the wings.
They help JETT-pup take off and land.

JULY 2   0 0 0 1 9 6 6   A.D.

PARKING

POWER

START

Starting Up

Starting up and flying the JETT-pup is easy. Follow these six steps before you take off.

1) Remove the wheel chock - it's the red wedge that keeps the JETT-pup from rolling away in case you forget to set the emergency brake.

2) Pull and release the parking brake.

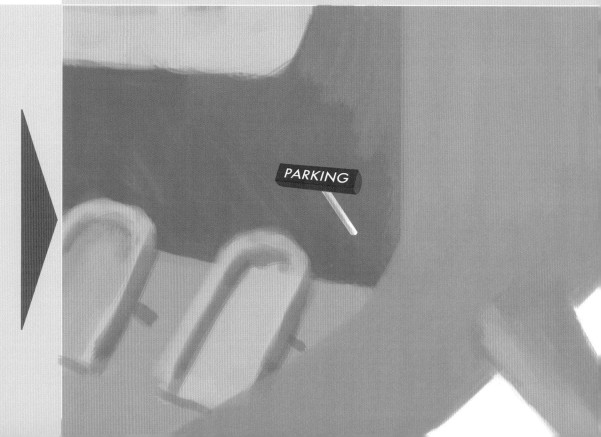

3) Pull the flaps back, to the DOWN position

4) Pull the throttle back, to the IDLE position

5) Flip the power switch up

6) Push the start button

You'll hear the engine wind up. Let it warm up for at least 2 minutes.

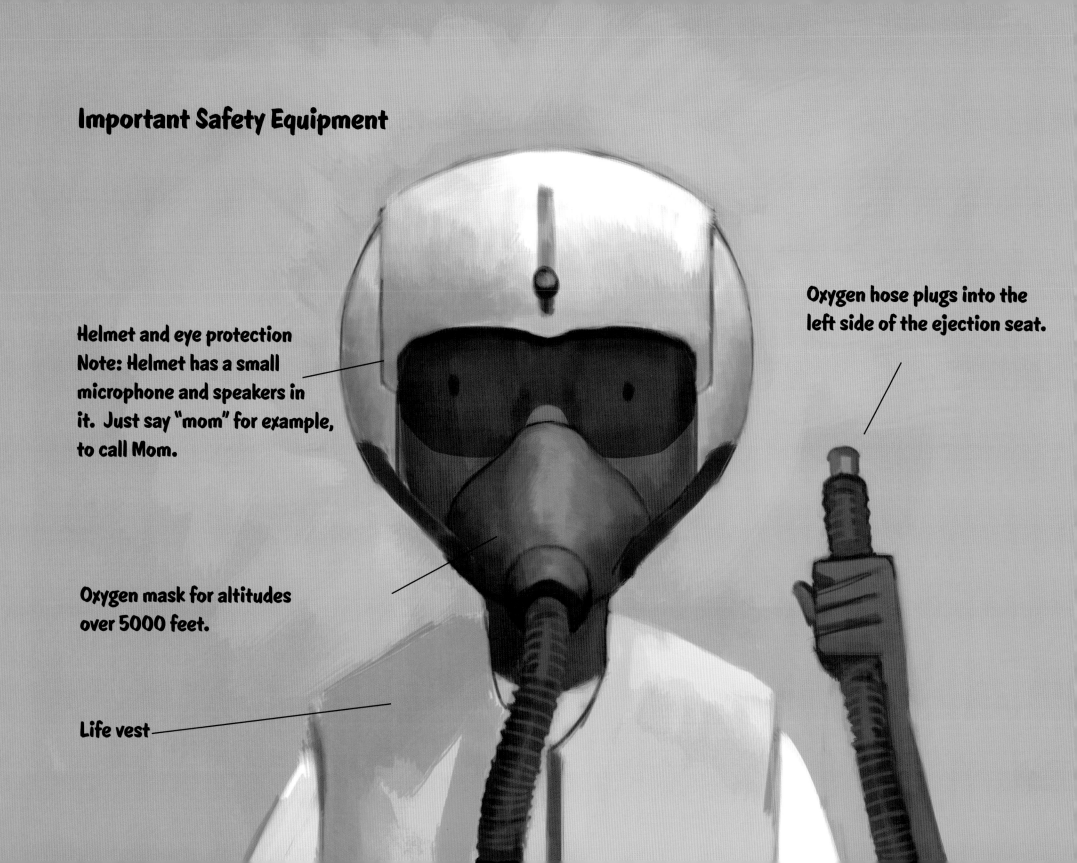

Important Safety Equipment

Helmet and eye protection
Note: Helmet has a small
microphone and speakers in
it. Just say "mom" for example,
to call Mom.

Oxygen mask for altitudes
over 5000 feet.

Life vest

Oxygen hose plugs into the
left side of the ejection seat.

Helmet and Mask come in various pet sizes

Small Dog

Large Dog

Cat

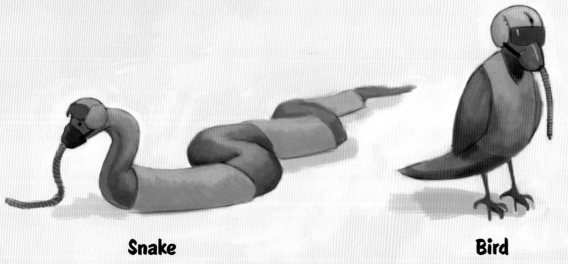

Snake

Bird

Guinea Pig

In the extremely extremely unlikely event of engine failure, push the EJECT button.

You'll be shot out of the JETT-pup like a rocket.

Parachutes will deploy for you, your pet and the JETT-pup.

If you eject over water, an emergency life raft will deploy complete with radio, snacks and blankets.

Important Safety Reminders

ALWAYS wear your seatbelt!

Don't forget your oxygen mask!

Watch for cars! Don't take off and land on busy streets!

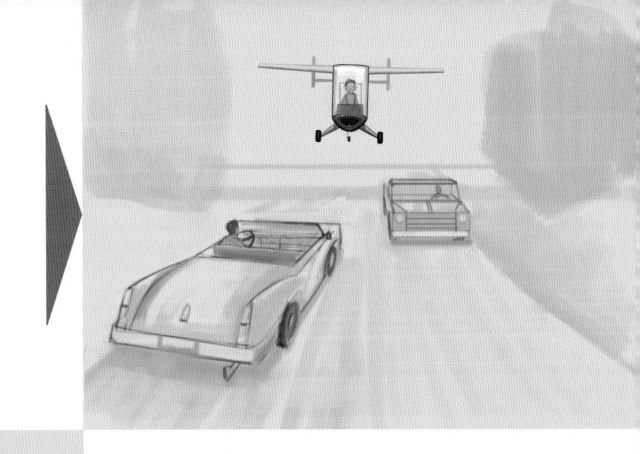

If you break the speed of sound at low altitudes, you'll break windows! Don't exceed speeds of 768 mph under 15,000 feet!

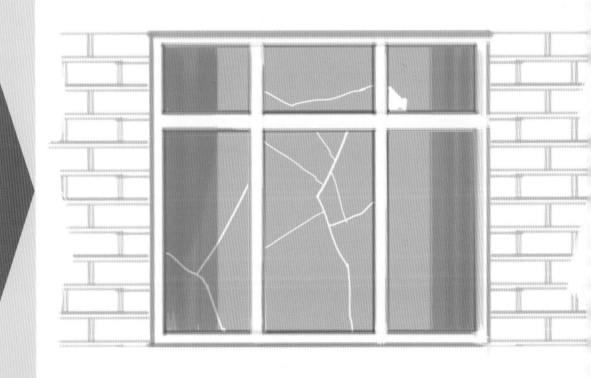

Taking Off

It's easy to take off in JETT-pup. Pull the flaps lever back (flaps down) and push the throttle forward to give the jet engine maximum take-off thrust. Once you're airborne, push the flaps lever forward (flaps up).

Basic Flying Maneuvers

Roll:
Move the control stick left and right to make the JETT-pup turn.

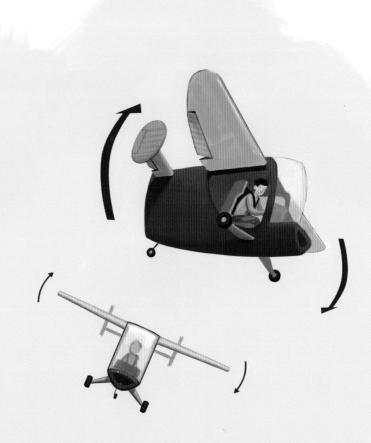

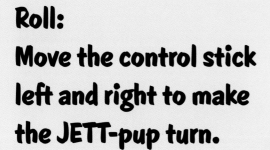

Yaw:
Push the rudder pedals up and down. This also helps the JETT-pup turn.

Pitch:
Push the stick forward or pull it back. This makes the JETT-pup go up and down.

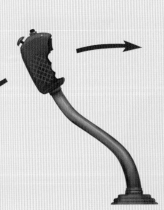

Landing

JETT-pup is easy to land. Pull the flaps lever back (flaps down), then ease back on the throttle, line up with the street and glide down. Watch out for cars! Always give yourself at least a block to land safely.

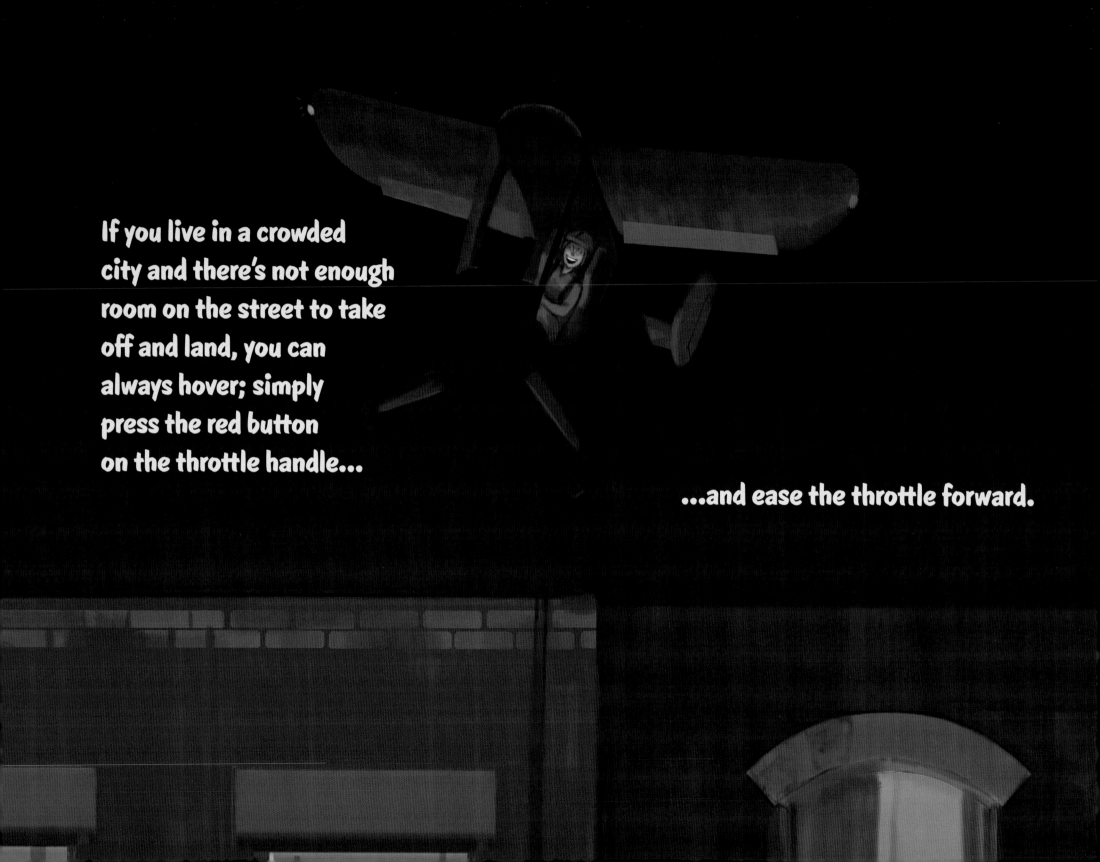

If you live in a crowded city and there's not enough room on the street to take off and land, you can always hover; simply press the red button on the throttle handle...

...and ease the throttle forward.

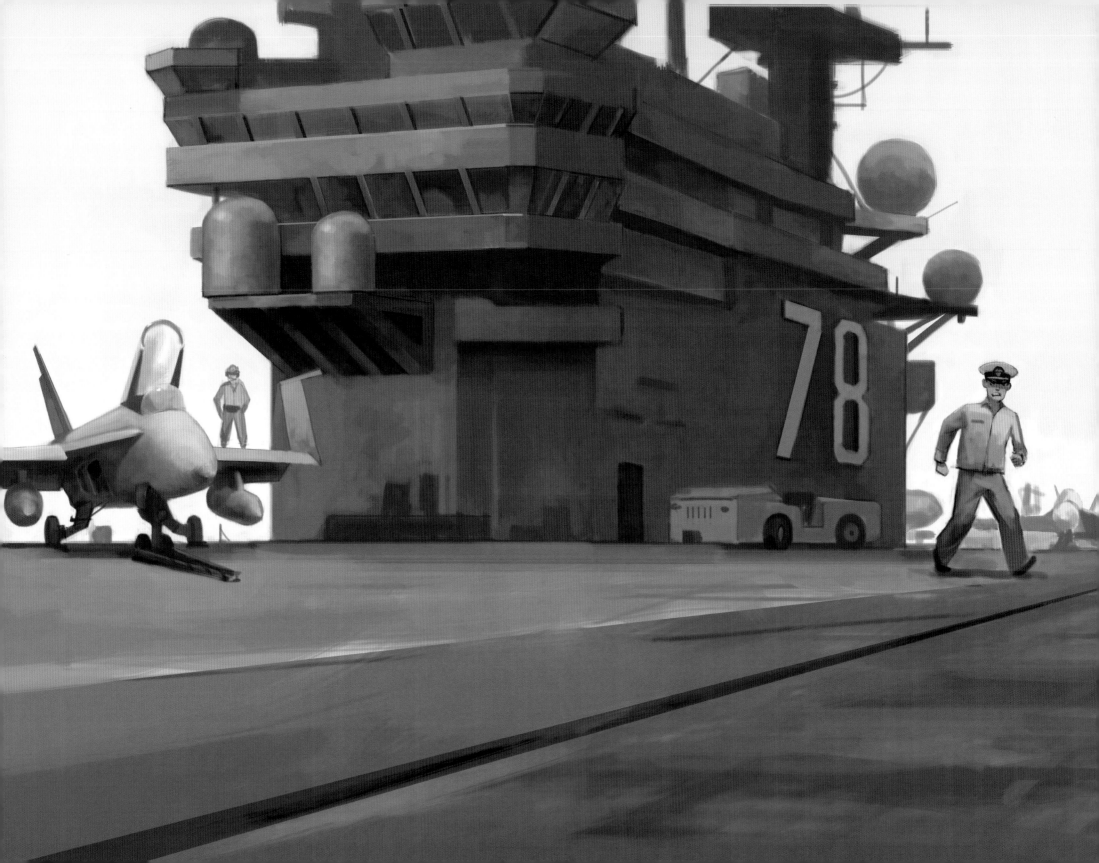

Important warning: NEVER land on an aircraft carrier. Especially without your seatbelt and helmet. You'll get in really really big trouble!

If you're time traveling back to the Cretaceous period (65-145 million years ago) DO NOT bring dinosaur eggs back with you...

...they WILL hatch!

Racing and Games
Attach pylons to your roof for racing...

Games

Balance an egg at the very top of a skyscraper!

Hook the mailbag!

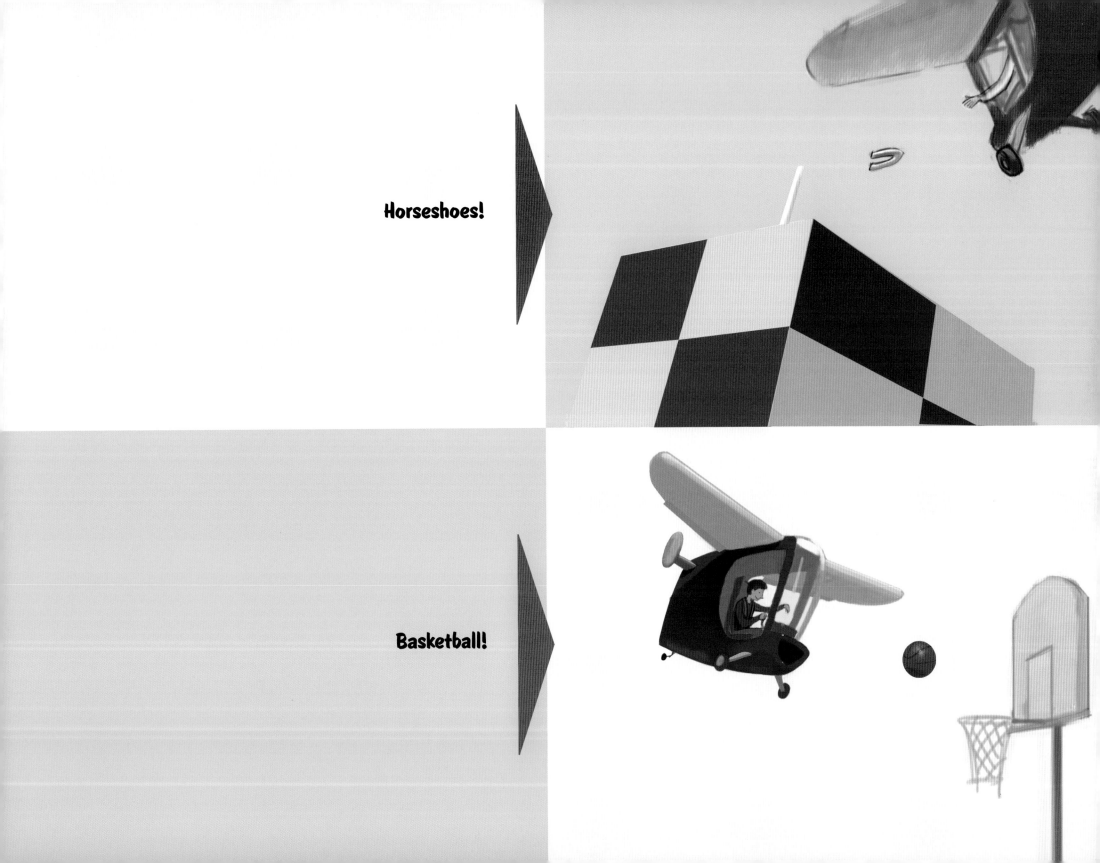

Horseshoes!

Basketball!

The Future

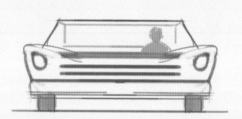

The Present

**The Wild West,
1860-1920 AD**

**The Medieval Era,
476-1400 AD**

Ancient Greece, 700-146 BC

Cro-Magnons, 35,000 years ago

Dinosaurs, 75,000,000 years ago

Formation of the earth, 4.5 billion years ago

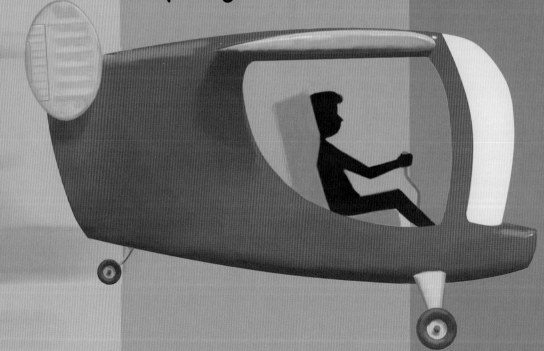

Some Time Travel Tips

It's best to read up on where you're going.

Be sure to see all the great architecture during the Roman era (150 BC to 146 AD).

JETT-pup's time travel generator won't allow you to go more than 99 million years into the future...

..or more than 99 million years ago.

Some Accessories

Stuffed Animal Gun

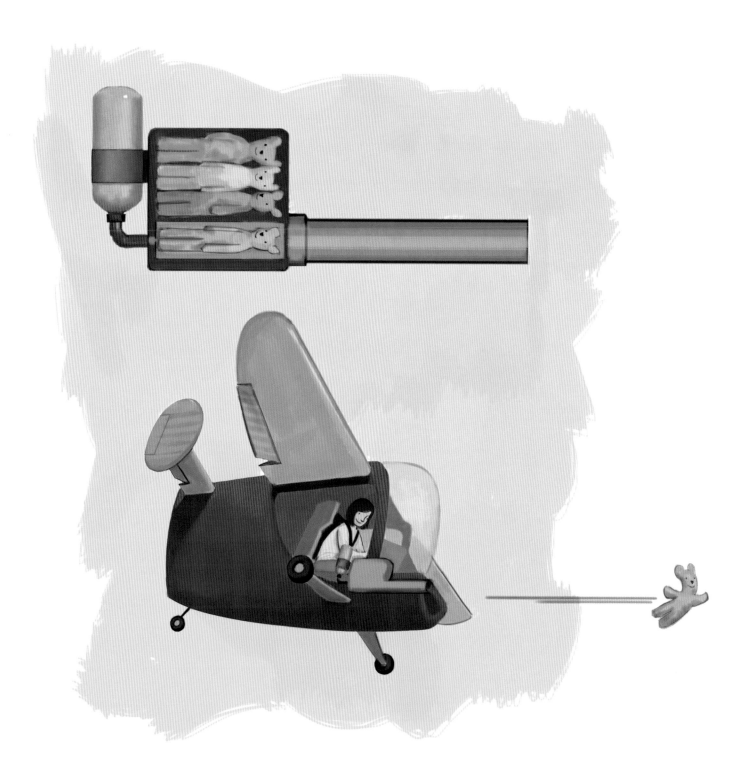

Tundra Tires to land on rough ground...

...and skis to land on snow.

Unicorn Rescue Harness

JETT-pup comes in a variety of colors.

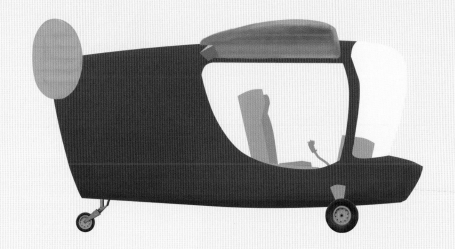

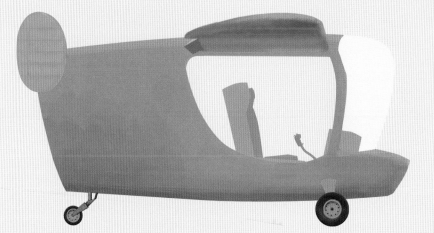

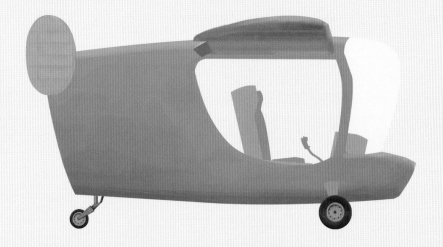

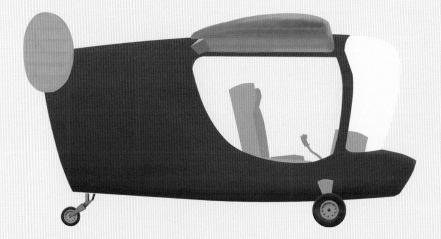

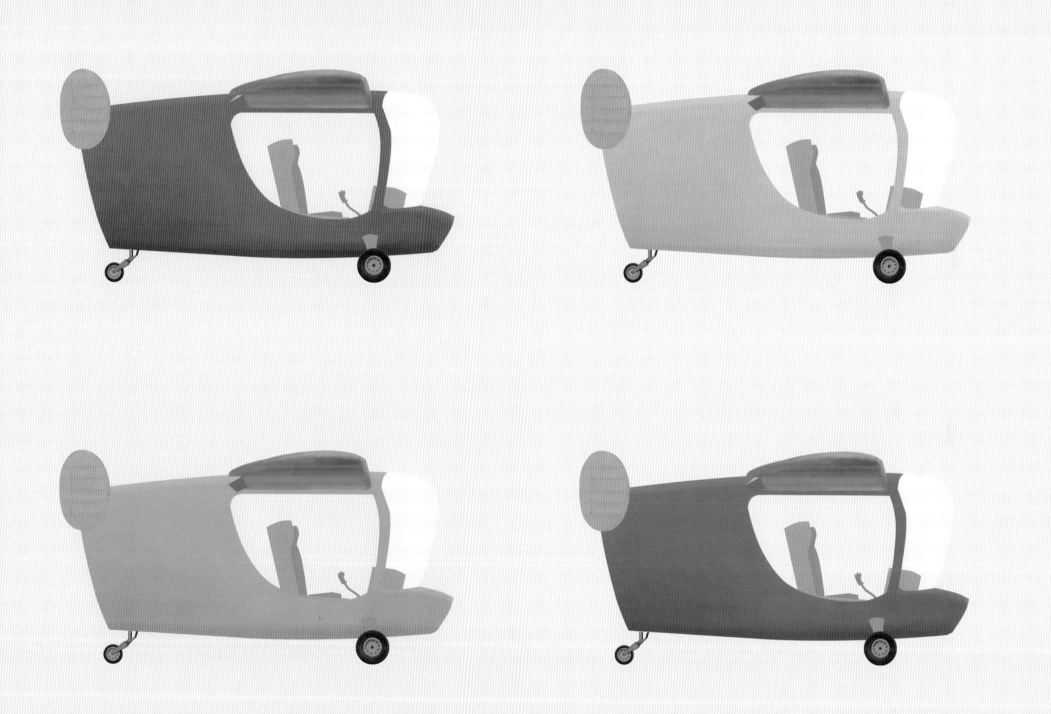

Fly safely and enjoy your JETT-pup!

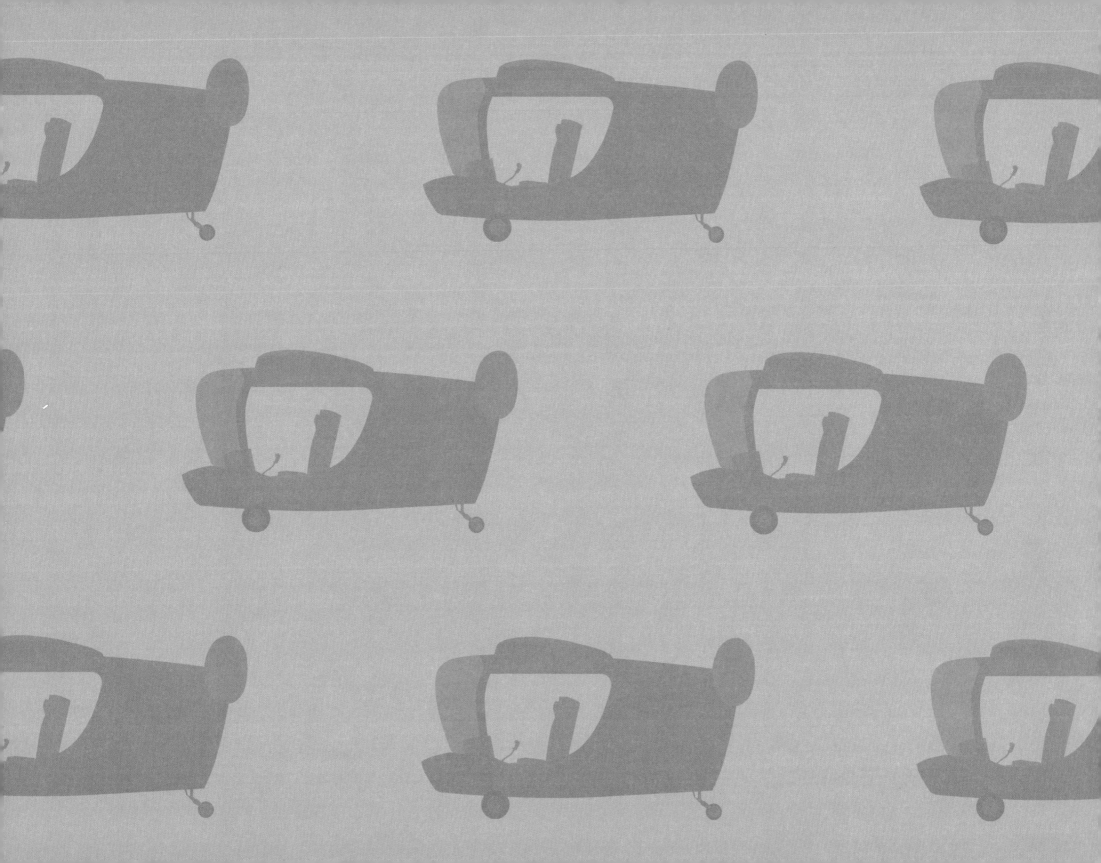